HOUSEBREAKING 747

MOHAMMED FAISAL.M

dedication

to my friends, teachers, family members and to the readers those who are reading it.

and especially to my class friends those who helped me to write this book.

Contents

Acknowledgements

acknowledgements

for all their insightfuls and their motivations for not leaving me to not to lose my focus on what i am doing. my special thanks to the editors, co authors and illustrators: ricco, niranjan, sudharshan, chris, alan, anton and rochan.

thanking my teachers and my librarian and my first on to my parents as they also sided for motivating me.

OTHER BOOKS

other books by mohammed faisal

faizalthefootballer

Preface

Mohammed faisal was born in 2009. he is actually a foreigner who was born in saudi arabia. he studied till his 4th grade and he came to india to become a footballer in his grade 6 he got three friends who are best called RHEA , ALAN AND RICCO.
faizal wrote this book with the writing inspiration of ponniyin selvan and he wrote this book to recollect the memories of the great INDEPENDENCE of India.

I

Everyone knows the army is a risky job of sacrificing the lives of their motherland. Knowing this, Jose joined the army when he was 19. He loves the militant and entertaining it, as his family members are also in the military, so his background is an army-coated one. In contrast, the generation of his family is in the army.

In 2025 he joined the International Army of the British.

But terrifying information is spreading among the IAB members "world war 3?".

The information was terrifying for Jose as he joined the army at a young and even though he entered, he didn't have the experience to attend world war 3.

But his face seems surprised and even shocked when he hears the news that "Jose! You are the TL of our team."

Now Jose is going to fight for his mother country, so he needs to be more and more trained and even train his Team Members. Such that Jose can fight in this war.

Jose is not the correct person to be a captain but one who can manage situations of variety. Jose usually likes to listen to songs at sunrise and sunset.

Jose laughs more. Even the laughter day didn't come. But he knows that laugh will turn a sequence in his life point.

Now, Jose is spending more on training himself and others too! It is march 21st, and everyone is getting ready for their night from 2 A.M.

Now it is 6:23 A.M.

Now Jose turned off the light of his tent and searched for coffee powder. Even though he found it, he nead steam water to mix and stir it.

jose usually loves football. he plays football in the sunset but as the time is 6 A.M. he just picked up his ball and called all his teammates for playing.

they all just played for 21 minutes and finally Jose threw the ball into his tent .

As the war is taking place in the forest areas and the army borders and more places.

Xavier now is calling Jose since it is getting time for the war ase it is 7:03 a.m.

Xavier is a chief commander who has the total control over Jose team.

Xavier will guide Jose for his more experience in the future war which is going to happen.

everyone is getting ready for war as is going to start in seconds of Justin

10 . Jose has a problem of having scariness.

Jose is still thinking of his family and his pet Julie. He loves his pet as she makes him happy whenever he is sad.

Jose and Rhea are close friends since grade 6; even she has joined the army with Jose as they both want to do something for

Their motherland. They both like each other as friends, but when the time comes for action, they will turn their concentration on their duty mode.

Rhea is a brilliant girl as she can think fast more than Jose. Even though she is more vital than Jose

Even she can run faster than him. Now, the whistle sound blooms from Xavier "soldiers assemble!"

The weather of the army land during the war was frigid to the extreme that each of the soldiers was getting fried in that hot. Six years went by this as the soldiers of both sides were getting an illness.

Jose is getting depressed about taking care of the ill soldiers. But soon they got well, and soon they participated in the war.

As soon as the sixth year passed, Jose got cut off his left limb.

When Jose gets injured, this news spreads to all countries in the war. So suddenly, Jose gets out of the war by Xavier as Jose gets an injury.

Now Rhea takes the captain position of the IAB army.

Months passed away like this Jose alos get quitted from this IAB job. He is trying for another job with his cut off limb

But he didn't get any jobs as he searched for many.

Natasha, a secret agent of NIA in INDIA.

Why India? Because Jose goes to his native home as his father get born there.

Natasha is a friend of Rhea; Rhea offered the agent vacancy offer to Jose

but Jose didn't accept the job vacancy offer as his injury stays still in life

But Jose doesn't know that this job will make him a hero in his life so that he will not forget something.

Rhea requested and even ordered Jose to join the vacancy.

Soon Jose got the idea of getting a duplicate limb to complete his leg.

Now Jose is going to the shop to buy it, and he brought it. Jose joins the NIA agency. After entering the agency, he suddenly got a task.

"task no:1 747". When Natasha blurts, Jose gets surprised as he doesn't herd the task name anymore. The first day of his task starts in the rise at 7 A.M.

Jose gets into the car and asks the driver to get to the Kerala airport.

Jose woke up very late at 6:45 A.M.

Jose suddenly got up and picked up his toothpaste, brush, and dress.

Jose suddenly changed his dress and brushed in the car, the driver doesn't know what was happening in the car, and he finally asked when Jose got down and stepped into the airport entrance," is my car a dressing ward or something else, sir? " Jose didn't answer all those silly ones. He directly got into the airport and gave his bag to the checking.

He takes off his bag from the checking mission, gets into the immigration area, and gets on the flight somehow.

It is an 8 hours journey and Jose, Rhea and Natasha are going to Australia

Jose saw something strange happening on the flight, But he didn't go extreme to notice that.

Soon the journey turned up to 2 hours to reach Australia. Suddenly a black t shirted man jumped on his seat and shouted to everyone, "everyone, put your hands up and heads down."

Jose got waked up

from his sleep. Jose asks Rhea what happened. Rhea shows her eye to Jose to see him up. Jose also saw up suddenly the black cat who was the robber, saying to him, "put your heads down and hands up."

Every passenger was confused about why the robbers were there and what they wanted from us. Now the robber reveals the truth by ordering"everyone! I and some of the robbers are here to steal the Cullinan diamond."

Natasha was joking are they don't know who is us. Suddenly the robber shoots her hand; Jose asks Rhea for the gun then Rhea throws the gun by slicing the flight floor. After getting the weapon, Jose shoots the guy who shot Natasha's hand. When he shot up the robber, the robber mistakenly shot the other robber and that robber who had AK 47 shooted everyone and finally he hit the roof of the flight.

Rhea runs to the Cullinan to save it. The robber even shot both pilots; now Xavier suddenly enters the cockpit to drive the flight as the flight is not in control right now. An unexpected shock and surprise for Rhea and Jose.

Natasha smells something that caught fire and is somewhere nearby her. she runs to the window of the left corner of the flight.

When she saw from the window inside she noticed that a fire was caught in the engine of both.

Rhea and Jose still didn't get out of the shock. Natasha shook both of their shoulders and said, Jose and Rhea, there is fire caught up in the left engine of both.

The robber, who is left right now, shoots Xavier, and he will die in a few seconds

now the flight turns up, slanting in the air. It's like crashing in the forest.

Everyone keeps their hands on their head and sits down on the flight.

Rhea alone holds the cullinan tight and sits down as soon as Jose open up his eyes he saw that Natasha got died and Rhea is in dizzy.

and started walking in the forest.